THEVELOC ITYOFCONST ANT

hardeep sangha

www.foxspirit.co.uk

The Velocity of Constant © 2014 Hardeep Sangha

Cover Art by Danielle Serra
http://www.multigrade.it/

conversion by handebooks.co.uk

ISBN: 978-1-909348-52-3

A Fox Spirit Original
Fox Spirit Books
www.foxspirit.co.uk
adele@foxspirit.co.uk

for deb

CLUTCHANDFLEX

suck a fist. extends down my
gullet. and then it spreads. i
can only break its arm at the
elbow to reciprocate my
love.

I'm fashioning my wired hand into a gun, resting the two fingered barrel into the dune of my temple. I cock the hammer back with my thumb, tonguing the roof of my mouth and letting it drop to provide an audible click. This feels safe, I can sleep like this. Of course when my mind crosses shallow waters to subconscious my feeble grip will relax, and that's usually when the nightmares begin and once again I am awake.

4:44AM/SIX FINGERS OF WHISKEY LATER

It elevates me propulsive like a bullet and I feel every ligament in my body flex, the sallow and inert shifting to make violent strides toward void. Clinging insects tumble.

The room is moving again, thick ripples moving outward from the framed painting of a crumbling tower in the centre of the far wall. I mute the TV and the familiar stutter of static from the wall rises, one for each ripple. On the TV Cliff mouths his words, regaling the bar with yet another useless fact, and as usual from the look on Carla's face she really couldn't give a fuck. I reach over for my notebook and flip back a few pages, striking through yet another row of lines on the one marked: Cheers.

'Every fucking time.'

I suspect the universe is trying to tell me something; coincidence took a powder 3 viewings of the same episode in... though I have no clue what. The shrill of the telephone, on the other end of the line Zoë[1] tells me to meet her at Denny's. I say I'll be there in 10 and close my eyes to let the now deafening static envelop me.

***

---

[1] zoë stands upon the bridge and its long diving stretch that leads out of town. tip toeing up to the railing she hooks her arms around two icy bars and peeks through, exhaling steaming air. a cigarette later and she turns and makes her way to the nearest phone booth.

A few local denizens are scattered around the joint when I enter, eyes fixed to their coffees, except Zoë who's scribbling furiously into her leather bound journal with a monocle pinched tight between eyebrow and cheekbone. Rachel[2] high fives me without looking up as I pass her table and slide into Zoë's booth, sitting across from her.

'Morning, Miss Shephard. And who may I ask is being bludgeoned with your penmanship today?'
'That prick, Mark[3].' she says, digging deeper into the page with each syllable.

Rachel told me how she'd accompanied Mark back to his apartment once simply out of boredom. Now, Rachel's teeth can cut a terse memory regurgitate like a wood chipper, with accenting saliva inking her hair in wild bursts, no carapace could hold those words and spittle, and I wouldn't nearly be able to do her brutal description justice, but start with a wall of bondage hoods and let your imagination work from there. She said, lazily rolling her eyes after catching her breath, that she had casually knelt on one knee and unzipped her left boot, producing a skinny black canister of mace, leaving Mark to drop dead weight and curl into the fetal position with both hands in a see no evil grip across his face. No doubt his eyes had been on the receiving end of a sting or two in the past, though that night Rachel never released a drop.

'If I hear the words *I told you so* escape from your lips... so help me god, Sean...,' slamming the journal shut and sending it, the pen and the just released monocle careening across the table and out the booth.
'Knuckle deep in my solar plexus, but I have a hold of its wrist, it will not get lost. Spread your palm.'

---

[2] rachel sits tracing never-ending circles around the rim of her coffee cup, waiting for the mime, who promised her the last of his velvet before he splits town, and recreating memories of her sister, kate, making sure to preserve every moment to its very last detail.

[3] bodies slide into one another. bass sends vibrations through arms all the way up to fingertips that reach to stroke it. black writhing silhouettes against pulses of burning yellow. an illuminated face winks and mark, taking a long pull from his beer, winks back.

Her glassy eyes strain not to blink lest that salty liquid drop and she tips the slightest of nods as the waitress slinks over and fills our cups, eyeing the journal as she pours.

'You kids ordering anything?'

2 BLACK COFFEES AND 3 CIGARETTES LATER

My decrepit building looms up ahead. Towering over me its walls are begging for a wet kiss, saliva to fills in those cracks, or perhaps just a hug. I'm reminded of a tree in the woods beyond the field where I played ball as a kid, with ring after ring of carved names that wound their way up its trunk. One day Zoë decided to climb it and I watched as she passed branch after branch only to slip and tumble to the dead leaves below. Standing over her twitching frame I witnessed her name etching itself into the still tree above, flakes of bark snowing down upon us and then running up our bodies in punching steps. Heel to toe, heel to toe. Into my navel, pushing up off my collar bone and gone into the air or someplace else, looking up I cannot see. Them's the brakes. For a moment the world distorts and I tighten the muscles in my torso, outstretching my skeletal arms to find something solid to hold onto, instantly creating fissures in the loops and whorls of my fingertips. It snakes inward toward the outside like clockwork, a machine. This damn sun is beating down something fierce and it'd be a colossal embarrassment to fall short of the stoop. I desperately need some sleep; coffee wasn't the brightest of choices. I pray Benny[4] is home and can help me out.

4 FLIGHTS OF STAIRS AND 5 POUNDING KNOCKS LATER

The scratching and scraping of the chain lock fixing and sliding into position and the horror flick creak of the door gradually opening... Benny's eye shivers into view with a rope of lank hair clinging to the corner of its lashes.

[4] the room has no gravity. in the centre the silhouette of a body lays suspended mid air, turning slow revolutions. a metamorphosis is occurring. synapses are firing and bolts of electricity are sluicing and cauterizing their way through the haunted, charcoal hallways of his mind.

'Who is it?'

'Sean.'

'Sean, who?'

'Sean, your fuckin' neighbour. C'mon, open the door.'

'Okay, okay. Jeez, enough with the profanity.'

Inside, Benny's apartment is identical to my own except for the clusters of monstrous words written with the many magic markers that lay strewn about the place. They've been appearing sporadically on the walls and ceiling over the last few weeks. I strain my eyes to make them out but give up after accepting the now permanent blur of my vision just isn't gonna budge.

'Anything of interest to report?'

'A spectacular head on collision. I boosted a car and was trying to get to Anna's.'

'No injuries I see.'

'My body returned before the moment of impact. Strange thing is I got a look at the other driver and I'm pretty sure it was me.'

'That... I have no response for that.'

'Yeah.'

'Anyways, I need some dream time.'

'Sit and relax, take a load off. Cheers is on.'

I dare not look at the screen, but the rote shards of dialogue have already confirmed it. Besides, Benny's not the most stable of persons and any more than 15 minutes at a time and it starts to show.

'I've already seen this episode.'

He shrugs and reaches into his pocket, fishing out a small amber vial, my eyes darting to the lupine shadows sifting the below around us from his movements and my own fibrillations. Flicking open the lid he pours half its contents out into his palm, fingering them around in circles in search of the right one. Finally he pinches the red pill free and tosses it in my direction. I catch.

IN MY PALM A BASEBALL BLACK LITTERED WITH BRAILLE AND BY SOME MIRACLE I FEEL AND KNOW EVERY WORD OVER ITS CONTOURS TELLING A TALE OF TWO LOVERS WHO LIVE ON AS BIRDS SHOT GUNNING ME BACK TO AGE 5 AS MY MOTHER LED ME THROUGH THE VERY SAME STORY HOVERING A FINGER OVER THE RELEVANT SECTION OF THE BLUE AND WHITE ILLUSTRATED CHINA PLATE AND DROPPING HER VOICE TO A WHISPER AT THE MOST ACHING MOMENTS LULLING ME TO SLEEP IN HER ARMS WHERE I DREAM OF ZOË AND I HAND IN HAND OUTRUNNING THE DISINTEGRATING SIDEWALK UNDER A SKY THAT HAS BURST A VESSEL PITCHING DROP AFTER DROP OF RAIN

4:44AM

The shrill of the telephone...

INT. DENNY'S
- NIGHT

ryan

    lowered tone,
stone faced stare,
gritted teeth and
my inevitable
reply:
    *'i'm a realist,
the dude had it
coming.*
    *he was a
clinger.'*

sean

    *'i gotta admit,
when they took
his body away, i
was as stiff as a
fuckin' board.'*
    and thought
to myself maybe
necrophilia is a
viable option.

beth

    *'some guy i
used to date
was found
dead, suicide.'*
    note to self:
    don't ever
let the world
see how
pathetic you
can be,
regardless of
the issues at
hand.

EXT. DENNY'S
- NIGHT

zoë

> 'you guys seen
> the mime?
>> i need some
> gear and no
> one's heard
> from that
> asshole in days.
>> know anyone
> who can hook me
> up?'
>>> i'm desperate.

rachel

> fuck the pigs,
> vampires are real,
> nowhere is now,
> gray is the color
> of choice, and
> i'm out of god-
> damn smokes
> again.
>> 'who knows.
>> maybe
> idaho.'

sean

> 'how much
> you need, zoë?
>> i know a
> guy.'

ryan

> 'who needs a
> ride?'

INT. RYAN'S CAR
- NIGHT

beth

as per usual the
world looks yellow,
even at night, urine
yellow washed
over the black.
'you really
think he
deserved that?
i know it was
only a movie, but
still...'

my iris burns.
it's this
yellow, it's
toxic.
i need a
parasol.
maybe the
dude did have
it coming, and
maybe i'm
enticed by
fear of
subtexts, but
tonight the
world is
yellow, and
for the record,
conversation
is dead.

leather skinned
sister from the ice
parade grips my
tongue with
serrated lips, the
aroma of burnt
knuckle hair on her
breath.

mr. mime is on
his street corner
being beaten by a
man with no eyes.

try and mouth
his prayer.

JEROMEearlier

jerome reprises
adaptation of
violent speak
disorder and
narrative revenge
lines for lucid
feast in high
resolution dreams
fuelling the
pristine opera

xi

*not something to
be swallowed and
detonated in my
interior, but to be
collapsed by.*

*it's easier to
walk when your
legs splinter, the
erosion of
jutting pistons,
protruding
bone and the
pain.*

*bite down and
weather it like
bad karaoke.*

*but no more
will i hate
disease ridden
cables running
the length of my
caustic spine,
as it curves
toward the last
monologue.*

*the word
embargo
exhibits
tomorrow,
nothing but
velvet and
viscera.*

*no post-
modern
distractions.*

take the case of porcelain:
her multiple personas each embedded with shrapnel for company...

& clean sheets for the pure morning after.

she's deleted, high on strings and bass.
no orchestra can relate the greek tragedy greater than ~~beth~~ when she's strapped and stripped in her blistered paragraphs.

10:26pm
there's archaic vulgar in sepia scattered in and around these bodies, stalking with murderous intent.

it's been a day and she's still warm.
take out my eyes.

hedonistic, sleep
deprivation's left me
anarchistic.
    this indolent
birth of wired
synergy clinging
to throat, six
shooter remedy
for a few lousy
kisses.

11:34pm
    and she's off
bartering for
meds, hair tied
back and
eyeliner
dripping.
    soiled
honey,
wet and
fierce.

insolent ophelia
is an outlaw with
dreadful dialogue.
    she dodges
bullets for
kidney thieves,
cigarette
clenched
between teeth,
screaming
obscenities at
passing kings
as she eyes the
ace of spades.

it works that
way with modern
romance, there's
almost no need
for the ever
dilapidating car
crashes of
yesteryear.

one

sexless trees make
you crave, and post-
coital sunspots are
heavenly when
exhaling the first
drag.

you'll sleep,
piercing genitals
with desolation.

hollow deities
packed in a brief-
case, ready for
the next day's
potential fiction
fight.

maybe liquor
date.

no trust, here we
blow prosthetic
middle finger kisses
when it rains blues
and reds.

lipstick nose-
bleeds contagious
on chemical
nights, a morning
buzz coupled
with electrical
lux.

fatalism works its
way through muscle
the color of red wine.

zirconia in hand.

thin, translucent,
anaemic skin.

and i'm ready to
cut class to catch a
beatin'.

parasite fishing
with no alluring
bait.

just a ring for
girl in idle
playground;
numb from
intricate detail of
self woven
fantasy, colliding
stars strapped to
frame.

she counts the
seconds till
december, thieving
my phallus…

binding me closer.

parched limbs and a
halo morning.
　dizzy cherub, still
weightless from last
night's love binge,
adorns fairy waste-
land with her all.
　'the minotaur stole
my fear,' she mumbles
to herself, deafening a
crowd of saviors.

walking backward,
gripping shoulders,
when eyes are weak.
　fleeting envy for
mannequins in their
agents uniforms on
nowhere street.
　the protesters at
the abortion clinic
never throw eggs in
my general
direction, but on
occasion paper
rocks and blades of
scented grass.
　they can see i'm
tied at the neck,
shirt creased.

this ain't subversive,
greek gods are dead.
　the cop smoked 'em
and cackled an evenin'
prayer.
　this is industry and
it ain't fiction.

it's all a substitute
for charred stills.
　they were burnt in
anger and buried
somewhere i cannot
recall.
　a medicated
holocaust.

still, brittle horses
never cease to amaze,
undressing to
flamenco sketches.
　each tonguing an
obol, ready for the
ferryman.

elsewhere, a drunk
preacher and his
feeble mother in law
have moved on.
　fuck 'em, they
never played their
music loud enough
anyways.

and the lorax <u>will</u>
have its revenge.

three

pack your bags my
structured heroine;
tonight we leave for
carelessness, leaving
tender uncertainties of
pain behind.

graciously we'll
decline the offer of
same abuse and
summer's solemn
complaints.

pretenders to
cynical world, on
the road to
assurance.

reconciling with a
lonely state,
retribution dame
plagues herself with
ignorance, a
collection of death
rattles held tight.

our questions
have no need of
answers.

sweet tedium.

i met her later that
night, club silencio,
she was dressed in
black.

we danced until
dawn, resonating
gravity like a head
trauma, then caught
a cab back to my
place.

there she ate me
whole after picking
my heart from her
teeth with a cocktail
stick.

no bullet wounds,
~~beth~~ hangs with pins
in her back, a mock
voodoo doll.

the next day spent
incognito, with a flick
of ash to enamour
disguise.

bodies double and
spines twist when you
regurgitate.

Q. 'you think we're
falling?'

A. 'faster, and it's
beginning to
wound.'

a message in a
bottle, lost in the
flow of my veins,
and open wrists
never seem to set
her free.
containing
rebel wishes,
centre of my
youth.

i'll sleep, deep
inside you, until i
drown.

we lynch strawberry
brats and draw blood.
hoping chaos
theories dull the
infants' minds
and swim
inconsistent,
sometimes
stopping to play
chess in the park.
she's 3 eyelashes
short of dominatrix,
guts and art, with rust
nails and a garish
ivory tongue.

there's familiar on
fingertips and a ring,
no other cinematic
image, only moments
of atrophy when her
ribcage imitates a
tenderness.
my rigid vertebrae
shatter after pulling
ripcord, a myriad of
meandering glass.

the poor tree's a
sucker for cig butts
and viscosity
dwindles faster,
tailgating vapid
dirge.
but i'm stealing
residuals of
eventuality from
spilt dreams, match
lit diaries from
around the time of
a funeral…

too much of her
in me.

are you heart?
city and all of
the above?
poker face or
not, lady luck's a
bitch.
never can tell.

stuck in paperback
mythology.
hourglass burnt
illustrations behind
text bodies.

it's always a matter
of deliverance, unsure
but sweet.
　　desperate
redemption
can be
visually
powerful, but
not stunning
enough,
m'dear.
　　i could never find
that perfect lie either,
my blood is ever
sadistic.

primal urges and
idiosyncratic
mauling, oedipus,
the creation ladder
effect.
　　or sometimes
just the scent of
paradigms on her
collar, stale as
solvent, dead as
disco.
　　and scorched if
symmetrical.

someone stone the
violin, this clown has
a berated frown, like a
killing spree in the
name of photogenic
cool.

belittle a lover for
argument's sake, it's
hereditary.
　　eventually i'll
tear open palms
and wonder if it's
a father figure or
simply a delicacy.

aggressive porous
sewn into ash for a
day make unrequited
horizons fragment
and lack.

she drew me a
sketch once.
　　it resembled
her.
　　she said it was
a portrait of me.
　　i gave her a
kiss.

jerome aged 5 has
sugar high and crack
in spine, maybe from
laughing too loud.
    i throw rocks at
his adolescence, a
tribute to ailments;
burn related
incidents,
destruction clocks,
and you in shades
of unclaimed blue.

it's the harrowing
gut wrench, soaked in
modern and vast
sculpture upon
sculpture, as clouds
fall, rolling from my
tongue.

    collapsing world,
time to start stalking
angels for
autographs...

or call in a
detective.

12:42pm
    a saucer of
whiskey was
put out for
rope veined
hands and an
ignorant
business suit,
not the cat.
    some fink
at a down-
town dive,
nursing his
endangered
home of
radius.

* * *

02:16am
    collar turned up,
inadequate midnight
king goes to work.
    first stop: the
leviathan himself,
mr. mime...

he just made my
shitlist.

six

the day spent teasing
a mime, reflecting his
every movement.
    finally, out of
frustration, he
caved and
revealed life's
secrets to me.
    'and how did you
obtain this
information,' i asked.
    'i spent 6 days
working as a spy in
heaven,' he
replied.
    'get the fuck outta
here,' i laughed.

there are animals at
the foot of my bed.
    one of them, the
lion, recites a
journal from my
childhood with
majesty and grace.
    another, the
serpent, sings
sad love songs.
    though, i laugh
rather than cry at
these, he has a lisp
you see.

    and then there's the
monkey, who simply
stares.

chess in the park:
    a panic war with
scarred gravity,
shedding its
confessions.
    we're rivals with
medication.
    make me up to
be a sidewalk
crack and shovel
those animals
inside, one by one;
i'll carry them as
an ark into the
earth.

there's no stability
in our language, just
the stutter of break-
beats.
    my rhetorical rib
itself clipped blind,
suffocating
mechanical lungs in
spiral hunt

    'it's your move,'
he whispers.

some say he lives
down by the wayside,
languid contusions
across his ornaments,
and yet not a single
insect is to be heard
cursing him out.

three moths circle
above worshipping
the artificial, my bed
sheets are still warm,
and sometimes i
lament gods for no
other reason than
habit.
lambs are easily
lead around these
parts, by letters
in braille.

to rotate the third
perspective and
align this machine's
lips with cables.
not acidic, but
familiar cables:

descending liquid,
anxious abortions.
i sleep in those
rivers, but not
amongst arrogant
imaginings.
there are maybe
19 torsos down
there barely
keeping afloat.
he uses them as
stepping stones to
my insides, it
doesn't hurt, but his
silence pierces.
stolen blueprints
to infinity tattooed
into the crevices of
his shallow pulse.

a formaldehyde
deluge is looming
over our overcast
skies.

but as ever i'll be
be preaching the end
of the world.
neon reverb.

i was in love with a
talk show host for a
week, before realising
the electricity in my
crummy apartment had
been cut off for over a
month.
    my television
projects predators
and poisonous
ink blots,
gangrene in my
charcoal third
eye.

it's never another
hollywood ending;
i'm forever caught in
a second act loop, a
temperamental sense
of raw incomplete.
    and my stinging
iron lobes are lazily
dripping trash.

    these feelings are
scientific, or maybe
retro golgotha with
its swollen herds and
silicone sweat.

jean-michel and i
gaze upon SAMO©
in his youth,
crowning the city
streets.
    i've heard the
pushers are
playing bach
down there, more
power to 'em, my
girl needs a hit.
    she complains
of methadone
blues.

paint me a portrait,
crudely rendered; i'll
sell myself for a dollar.
    my marble palms
they itch,
switchblades pillaging
absence.

    this hour is harsh,
we've almost
diminished, no man's
land appears out of
reach.

    last train leaves at
midnight, i'll meet
you on platform 4
with wilting red rose
in hand…

trust in me.

Q. 'how much you
need?'

A. 'gimme a gram
of velvet, i got
the itch.'

some dialogue
recluse and i
writhe.
we are lovers.
the crack in
his left cheek
adjusting as we
fuck in snap
shots of
atrophy.

lacerations to
heart, body
flawless.

there's a claustrophobic
hangnail in a high pitched
monstrous bend that strobes
cancerous bleached bone
bound in black cord and
satire.

it's all coming back.

here and there on the
mainline there's no other
but dust to kick and
scratch.

i knew this girl once
who sold sunflowers and
punk rock clichés on
street corners, her dream
was to save up enough
cash to build a trojan
horse.

she had this plan to
invade mexico city
after an acid fuelled
surge of kerouac's 242
choruses.

i don't know why,
but i miss those
sunflowers.

i wonder if she ever
made it.

orphaned sibling of
delirium, rogue to
symphony of sarcasm,
with her usual diet of
coffee and nicotine.

on the 7th day we'll
meet, final masse, and
discuss the destruction
of ambient cell.

maybe even listen
to some jazz and
worship textures.

i smoke cigarettes in
high heels clutching a
gas mask.

i am a golden god.

pity merchants have
no eyes, this talk is
nonexistent.

we tread the streets
of warsaw, hand in
hand, unearthing
monoliths.

ten

the winter sun swallows
rhythmic connect with
endearing rabid hunger,
heartbreak from pacifying
dogma days.
but i'll overcome this
heresy, one petal at a
time.

and it begins: no more
abstractions, no more
pornography. check into
motel room, date with
pilate at midnight. need a
shower; teeth are rotten,
bland and gray. the
bastard kneels to detach,
shotgun in hand, frail
veins in tow. a thousand
ballads in constant
reprisal. only once, only
twice. revolutions for
apathy. ~~beth~~ is singing
lullabies hours until dawn.
give me the third on
desolate highway with no
strange demons to speak
lies and riddles. let
paranoia sleep tonight, his
collarbone is a nexus to
nowhere. after kisses we
make love, terrible
moment speaking in
tongues. but roses are still
red and violets are always
diseased. take two spoons
of sugar, razor blade
hope, and pray for
substance. it's hunting
season, go go go

an ingrown oak tree,
root and tip buried, its
menacing bark as
crippled as its bite.
under it we sleep,
for what seems like a
millennia.

crooked illusory
dreams.

as kitsch as hours,
the rodent's cheap
malaria like scent
loiters the arcade.
    some castrated
cat leers.
    its optics drone
alchemy.

'i can craft
fractures into
your torso,
finger trace
the left ribcage
into eggshells,
but triads are
converging
and there's no
time for
pillow talk.'

dissecting
specimens
has become
cliché, and
attempts at
aborting
rippling veins
arbitrary.

SCENE MISSING
0062048

04:23am
    time to kill till
sunrise: 3 hours.

no marxist ever
spoke as glib as
that urchin, not
even my valentine.

only carbon
monoxide thrills
are absolute,
swallowed with
milk.

but not on this night,
with its gouache moon
held up high and
stretched wide using
safety pins.

rowing argonauts
have lost their way:

a fluid emotion
sprawl as flexible
as my progress in
scribbles of
ancient phone
conversations for
orbiting planet's
mathematical
visuals scrawled
across the absurd
& irresponsible

deep within the
bowels of dunes
and constellations,
third from the sun,
on the road to
damascus, the
vanishing point.

pagan sands and a
distant déjà vu, slim
pickings from the
coma patient.
i know the punk's
fakin', just waiting
for a violent wink.
but, he left his
briefcase in the
underworld, it's a
cinch he's fucked.
the backlit swan
dive was for
nothing.

give me a break-
beat, i'm surfacing
sinew and cartilage,
taut migration
distances to sterile
years.
and this is just
another mean jive,
never nostalgia.

metropolis feed-
back plunges
affection into
diabetic alienation
wrists.

07:48am
the dirty sun and i
imitate a tenderness.
coming soon to a
theater near you, like
a sucker punch.

**BETH, YOU IS
MY WOMAN
NOW**

sleeping to
vicious beats,
no sleight of
hand.

INT. DENNY'S
- DAY

rachel

what's a girl
gotta do to get a
fuckin' refill
around here.

*'so, you
finally
checking
outta this
dump, huh?'*

the mime

'i guess so.'
not for
sympathy,
nor the
tangles
above his
nape.

rachel

'where to?'

the mime

'wherever.'

rachel

mother,
rorschach,
placebos.
*'i hear
idaho's
nice.'*

EXT. DENNY'S
- DAY

rachel

    *'you gonna
tell me what
happened to
your face, or
do i have to
guess?'*

the mime

    'guess."

rachel

    *'someone
beat the shit
outta you?'*

the mime

    no time for
pillow talk.
    *'you stay
cool, rache.
    i'll catch
you on the
flipside.'*

rachel

    *'peachy
keen,
jellybean.
    you
know
me.'*
    need to
pick up
smokes.

INT. MIME'S
- NIGHT

the mime

    ...

OBJECTS IN
MIRROR ARE
CLOSER THAN
THEY APPEAR

BETHlater

7

IT STARTS WITH A BREATH

guts into thorax to complicate
cruel conceited collisions of rigid
structure and delicate muscle that
brawl with my throat for expired
lungs as they revolve in spun
detail of an aperture bursting
scalpels whilst being crushed by
gravity to sketch and exhale this
my sacred violation machine
secretly outlining clouds with
fingertips in hopes of exploding
cities in heaven a block at a time
because fuck ethics i say

several sparks in my eye line
appear drowsy maybe medicated
as they collapse and lilac ghosts
are snapping their fingers to
some fictional beat sound
tracking my strides across main
street carrying a crystal bow
shoulder slung for ill tempered
survivors with fury clasped in
each of my fists preaching solar
sermons on orbiting satellites
the mighty gods of our time even
though rachel says *beth, you're a
dreamer* and that the runs in her
stockings are caused by
vibrations from natural disasters
in faraway lands no man dares to
venture

LATER THAT NIGHT

illusory thieves are holding a
candle light vigil for the last of
the magical creatures that inhabit
our collective conscious and i'm
sledge hammering my imaginary
walls demanding they *keep the
goddamn noise down* but i'm
also curious as to what somber
departing words this beast may
have to offer and decide to pack
my cigarettes and take a
vacation as the details of my
decaying apartment and its
surrounding world descend into
some lame parody of a lynchian
nightmare any hormonally
challenged youth worth a nickel
would be proud to imitate

12

JUST ANOTHER BURIAL

for the record there are three
hundred and fourteen souls in
attendance which include the
usual freaks and geeks as well as
rachel and myself under a sea of
ashen umbrellas on account of a
distressed sky dealing with
issues none of us could really
give a fuck about when on cue
some dame behind us lets out an
agonizing howl that would break
the heart of even the meanest of
grade school kids and screams
murder as a glossy gray casket is
lowered into dirt as dark as birth
prompting rachel to turn and
quizzically whisper into my ear
is this what passes for love?

JUST THE FACTS, MA'AM

a crooked smile, the son of a
bitch had a crooked smile, with
a blaze of gritted metal teeth
etched into the folds of a black
hooded cloak

5

PICKING UP SMOKES

as per usual the raven haired
clerk offers me a subversive rant
on the dangers of a warm but
parched simplicity and its
disruptions of attraction and the
subsequent euphoria and as per
usual after seconds of silence on
my part she grins and tosses a
pack of luckies in my direction
licking *on the house* with a wink
and a claim of a former life as a
contortionist before scrambling
over the counter wielding a
shotgun for the diseased punks
in the back of the store stuffing
birth pains under skinny shirts
whilst cocking a round into its
keen but equally lonely chamber
poised for the inevitable bloody
standoff as i spark up a smoke
and exit the joint whistling the
theme tune to that show about a
gal named lucy

OUTSIDE

a tedious sun hangs like a
clouded ring of burning
embers

45

doctor burroughs' hollowed
sockets edge their way from my
dilated pupils to some fixed
point in space to the right of my
brittle bass pounding skull as i
sincerely machine gun another
idly thought out tale of inspired
confidence when in my
periphery i notice spirals of
nomadic smoke feverishly
tailgated by waves of cerulean
flame spreading like vine over
clinical olive realizing as our
hallucinations converge that the
good doctor and myself are in
fact one - concluding the static
session with the usual treat of a
kola flavored sucker and an
always comforting *i think we've
made a lot of progress today,
miss wells*

DETAILS

the summer of my seventh
year i stood knuckle deep in
burning green grass with my
eyelids sewn together tight by
the afternoon sun and
engraved a message to my
future self to remember that
that summer of all the
summers past was the greatest
and to this day i can dissect
that lone moment to its very
last detail though not a single
other second of that summer
exists for me

BENJAMIN AND I

    for the record it's thirty three
ominous steps to benny's
apartment door where i enter to
find him violating his walls with
crucifixes and garlic whilst
shattering holy water over
blistered windowsills and lining
his skeletal torso with clips of
silver bullets to be held in place
by shards of black masking tape
he's torn with jagged incisors
and hung in an ever expanding
spiral upon an overcast arced
ceiling clutching a dripping
chandelier that reflects and
scatters a fiery kerosene yellow
across my sterile profile as i ask
whether he's finally lost his
mind to which he replies *maybe,
but isn't that the point? i was
birthed from a bohemian womb*
and i nod in agreement before
inquiring whether he has any
decent gear on him as my regular
dealer the mime skipped town
last week

I CONNECT

    in skin to skin bruising and
the collecting of abattoir
obituaries i see correlations
and constellations and they're
running electrical wiring like a
nerve network between me and
the winter air

as per usual rachel trounces
me in our best of three battle of
rock paper scissors and begins
with a tale of a former
classmate who's otherwise
immaculate penmanship
regularly scrawled twisted ink
fuelled arteries along a forearm
to be nicked at a later date by
broken glass and smoothed over
tight with layers of petroleum
jelly which she blissfully called
her mock ritual to indulge a
combusting world and i had
planned on following this up
with a hideously cynical
diatribe on the moral plight of
the human vertebrae only to
suffer rachel's continued tirade
of abhorrence for the
aforementioned classmate to
which i sigh *just let it go*
committing to memory for the
record that there are no visible
clouds surrounding a perfect
luminous moon tonight

I DETACH

there is a horse vermillion in
color and sculptured in form
under a bitter serrated sky where
i sit gripping rachel's frame
nestling her frozen features into
my neck as her wrists fall limp
and the horse comes apart meat
through tendon silently slipping
the three of us into sleep

ELSEWHERE

here i am toothless grinding
my gums with slick hair pulled
violently back and intricately
woven into the watery cables of
a pulsing blood red womb
where time is sinuous

5

JUST ANOTHER SIBLING

tangles of gnawed souls blur
past in quick succession door
after door on ward thirteen
where the air reeks of singed
hair and formaldehyde the
aroma of the deranged a word i
lament using after an hour of
frenzied searching and
eventually finding kate down a
curving stairwell leaning her
pallid features into a splintered
windowpane whilst swallowing
a burn from an unlit cigarette
rachel slipped her last visiting
day seemingly strung out on the
drizzling rain encompassing her
eye line and mumbling
fractured syllables that carefully
quiver *i haven't seen snow like*
this since we were kids, you
remember, bee? you, me and
rache? flicking the dead
cigarette and exposing a trail of
crimson migrating down a pale
arm as a pack of nurses rupture
the moment and wrestle her to
the ground against the sound of
screams

DRIVE

tangles of gnawed branches
blur past droning atonal as ryan
grimly recounts the day he
massacred a nest of vulnerable
insects in his youth that coils its
way to my ears as a lullaby
amassing the menacing
daydream now peering into the
passenger side window looming
over my reflection

FOR THE RECORD

i can remember the snow as
well as the three bodies below it
tiptoeing to catch bludgeoning
flakes with outstretched tongues
like acidic communion wafer on
a calloused sunday morning

this one could use a fucking chemical peel he announces savagely scrutinizing the feeble contours of some dame trapped within the sardonic borders of a canvas and raising en route the eyebrows of a few disgruntled denizens who throw blunt daggers in my direction imploring me to exert some kind of restraint only to hit my usual self inflicted vacant expression as i secretly curse myself for bringing ryan along with me but hey i needed a ride which is what i keep repeating to myself as he further adds *and a wax, the eyebrows on this bitch, jeez*

STANDING MALE NUDE WITH RED LOINCLOTH

as per usual an amalgamation
of fear and fascination swims the
length of my spine as i approach
him suspended upon his wall with
barbed wire taut over aching
clavicles shrieking skinny vain
stillness and surface precision in
a stuttered disparity of tides and
opulent wounds feeding reckless
mescaline instincts that lack
delirium but perversely stretch
molten muscle sickness strewn in
disarming trembles to make a
patchwork of something abstract
lingering in neon long enough to
endure those salient tendrils
scraping at indifference whilst
subsiding what i covet for he is
my awkward angel disillusioned
and alluring

ANATOMY

there is no conflict nor reflex
when i extend my left arm and
surge internal pressure to free it
from the ligament and muscle
binding the second joint it simply
dislocates and continues on its
sullen path arriving to stroke the
razor ridge of my shoulder blade
with blind fingers

he starts by breaking off the
legs grasping it by the back and
tearing them off with a twisting
motion before moving on to the
arms ripping them off at the first
joint again with a brutal twisting
motion using a wrench to break
off the hands revealing raw
meat and bone which he grinds
with splitting knuckles out
through the opened shoulders
sleeving his bulging forearms
with residual skin in the process
as he grasps the tail section with
one hand and the back with the
other and twists to sever the
segments in two inserting
knuckles again to drive meat
bone and viscera out through
twitching breaches - concluding
the sadistic gorging with the
usual treat of two plush
monthly checks a tip of a hat
and a cold *g'night, kiddo* that
hangs in the air long after he's
departed

INSIDE

plumes of this derelict town
unwind and scatter into the
hanging waters above

4

COFFEE AND CIGARETTES

interior denny's restaurant day and rachel skips in whistling the theme tune to that show about a bar where everybody knows your name seating herself across from me as the following conversation rapid fires within extreme leone style close ups beth: *so, how was your date?* rachel: *ugh, the guy was a freak, he made mark seem well adjusted* beth: *and...* rachel: *and i maced the fuck and took a powder, just like you taught me* beth: *atta girl* rachel: *you get my check?* beth: *y'know, you're gonna have to see him sooner or later* rachel: *no time to spare, i'm heading out on an epic road trip to cure the world by means of infanticide* beth: *sounds like a plan* rachel: *why, you in?* beth: *sure* rachel: *great, cause we need to break kate out on the way* beth: *that we do* i nod gravely in agreement *that we do*

FADE OUT...

i stood and stared
at my wrists for the
longest time today,
noticing some
discoloration.
  *'purple... yeah,
definitely some
purple.'*
although, the
three banshees
on my front lawn
had kept me from
sleep again last
night, maybe i'm
seeing things.
  it was clear their
mohawks had grown
considerably longer
since the last time i
peered behind
closed curtains, still
refusing to make
eye contact.

they sleep by day
curled in fetal
positions.

  taking off was
the right move, the
bitches refused to
vacate, and
another night of
those screams was
damn sure out of
the question.
  but this
purple...

  here comes a car.
  *'about fuckin'
time.'*

'...when roots are
torn all that's left is
the velocity of
constant,' he replies.
'amen, brother,'
i say.

judging from his
expression i suspect
this isn't the correct
response and avert
my gaze to
momentary images:

a jack-knifed oil
tanker, a burning
barn, a field of
warring cattle etc etc

there's nothing
ahead but a line
separating the road
from gunmetal
gray clouds that
resemble
orphanage interiors.

a lone white horse,
emaciated and aflame,
gallops past and into
the distance.
i need sleep, this
road blurs.

my driver and i
split a cigarette
whilst surfing
stations for an ideal
soundtrack, finally
settling on some
pixies.

break my body,
hold my bones...

daylight dims and
i'm scarcely seconds
into my delusion
when they appear,
those three fuckin'
broads.
      coils of charcoal
smoke drifting from
their pouting, tar
black lips.
      i wave and get a
scowl from each in
return.

i know this place,
this beach; i was here
aged five.
      some kid with a
mean streak broke
my arm for kicks.

      trailing the shore-
line, i find the
snaggletoothed fuck
building sandcastles
and i…
      'wake up, kiddo.
we're here.'

WELCOME TO YET
ANOTHER UNDER-
WORLD POPULATION
51,201

i'm not sure why
i'm still with him,
but he says he's glad
for the company,
and for a crushing
moment i ache from
simply being
wanted.

      'this town looks
bleak.'

59

'this, my son, is the
cadillac of pies,' she
says with enthusiasm i
can't even begin to
comprehend.

the *son* remark
throws me, and for
the briefest of
moments i
contemplate
enquiring whether
there's any truth
in the claim.

until of course i
notice her hair and
decide there's no
fucking way any
mother of mine
would be caught
dead wearing a
rainbow scrunchy.

still, i dig her zest
and order coffee &
pie for me and my
new companion.

'some stale faces
in this joint,' he
mumbles, and i know
just what he means
there are vultures
perched on the
shoulders of each of
these patrons, just
itchin' to pluck out
an eye.

'guess we'll fit
right in.'

the motel air is ripe,
sickly sweet, like old
war tales and the scars
that accompany them.
 and as midnight
closes in on us,
you'll find me
sitting upon a
windowsill, arms
locked around my
knees, fetal, staring
out at my banshees,
who are forever
shackled to my
wrists.
 my friend will be
lost in tides of sleep,
his torso rising and
collapsing, barely
audible breaths
acting as a sound-
track to the lull.

 outside they'll be
whispering mantras,
and i know the name
on their lips.
 i'll smile, giving
'em the finger and
blow them each a
kiss, unable to
contain salty tears
from striking my
skin.

goodnight

 i'll mouth the
word, but not a
syllable of sound
will escape.

the man in the
moon puffs on his
cigar, and the stop
light at spark-
wood & 21 stays
red.

CODA

silas knew the tiny, winged creature was real, although when he would reach out for it with his mud-caked, little palms it would flicker, distort and disappear. he considered telling his mother of his new find, but just yesterday she had frowned on his insistence of a nativity scene coming to life and he didn't want to push his luck. besides, the miniature joseph and mary standing over the sleeping baby jesus - who only pretends to sleep - were sure to bicker and argue again soon and he didn't want anything to detract from his glorious victory when they did. he could tell his brother, nathan, but he wasn't around. in fact, one of the kids from the yard next-door had asked him just the other day whether he thought nathan had gone to heaven or hell, to which silas replied 'nah, i'm pretty sure he's out getting milk. ol' nate loves his milk.' the kid simply stared and inside silas felt a crushing weight grow heavier and heavier, like hot, pooling liquid rapidly congealing. there was an image to accompany this weight once, but he never could make it stable.

we argue over the littlest things. i shot her once, but only her shadow felt the sting. a black void of outlined features snapping back as the bullet pierced its temple. it's been lying in our apartment since that day, slumped in a corner, becoming more and more defined each time the sun approaches the horizon. i hardly notice it anymore, though from time to time a dinner guest will point out how fabulously post-modern the crime scene is and i'll exhale a crushed sigh. miriam, on the other hand, furiously performs mouth to mouth on the corpse each night. i watch her, tip toeing out of bed, secretly pumping its motionless chest in a panic, only to find claustrophobic air. she wants to be whole again and i'm not sure why i do not want her to be. when her adrenaline is burned she gives in, sliding back under the covers, exhausted and out of breath, and i imagine each violent lungful is a bullet to the back of my neck. tomorrow i'll bury and mourn, even though i'm certain her severed half will refuse to budge, or we'll just argue again. the two are one and the same.

MIRIAM'S BODY

BENJAMINagain

A dripping faucet is ringing in her head, acidic against her frontal lobe, as she wades through currents of tall grass to the spot where she stood and carved juvenilia into her inner walls many years past. Her sister is there to assist, whistling the theme tune to a long dead sitcom and aimlessly hacking at the shifting growth in an attempt to clear a pathway for her struggling sibling.

She births him standing upright, after nightfall, and rabidly chews the umbilical cord free with her teeth, naming him Benjamin after his father who died prematurely within the folded wreckage of a car.

Sinking to her knees, she blows a kiss into the swallowing air as her sister cradles the newborn and howls at a glowing, bloodshot moon.

This is zero.

I'M RUNNING, nondescript, between cold symmetry. out here, in the absence of towering structures, a design is visible. i don't know whether to take comfort in that or knife the horizon at a vicious angle. the night, as ever, is long, with no clouds to create creatures and no star either.

THERE ARE no imaginary lines when i wake, only the real, and it washes over me with sight, scent and sound. the bathroom mirror distorts my reflection as my eyes adjust, patches of convulsing stubble. outside, when i trail crawling amputees they moan, writhing as i approach, they're migrating and my heel is an atrocity upon their ears. sore leaves clutter the yard and penetrate underfoot.

i see her[5] every now and then at this time of day, naked arms limply crossed on a ragged couch - which has been dying a slow death on her peeling porch as far back as i can remember - staring at some fixed point in space with a cigarette dangling from her dry, bitten lips. over the years i've come to admire the scars upon her skin, the spirals snaking over her wired form. in my youth i would fret at the sight of my own blemishes, stark aberrations afloat on a sea of bland, amongst the faintest of ripples. but there's comfort in these constellations now and i look forward to the next. i'm a collector, and hers appear so defined and intricate. i drag the minutes sipping my coffee, hopeful to catch some new movement; to see those scars animate. but she remains still.

[5] when eloise was nine she caught a dragonfly in a honey jar. she poked holes in the lid with a biro so it could breathe and studied it for hours. her brother, silas, observing eloise's wonderment, snatched the jar and pen in a jealous rage and stabbed the insect. eloise shed many tears, but kept the speared corpse hidden under her bed, wrapped in a red handkerchief. years later she would carefully remove the biro and write a poem for a boy in her class whom she had developed a crush on.

4:44pm

A MAN[6] with digital skin strikes up a conversation on the train today, relaying his question to my blurred reflection in the passenger window. after some thought i send his echo a reply:

i don't know really... um, it's like when you puncture an apple... and it exhales smoke, you know? knots of smoke that form palms and fingers. you see them clench and bloom and it reminds you of pistons at work, the mechanics of a day. but it's also another language and you're instinctively aware that something is lost in the translation, so you take another bite to subside the confusion; this time to the bone. often i'll tear into the arch of her throat and i'll shiver... numbers do not create these cavities, there's no mathematics involved... in a religious way, i'll shiver. it's autoerotic asphyxia, a nail bomb, assimilation... insects in my limbs.

his features, they tighten, surfacing a network of circuitry from beneath, and it begins, spatters of dead pixels appearing here and there, savagely erasing each protruding cheekbone with momentum. i turn and watch as he sits silent and still during this consumption, and blow a kiss into his void before exiting at my stop.

---

[6] to his recollection, david has never been in love, though over the years several girls have delivered the words to him in earnest. some whispered, some screamed, and one wrote them in a poem to him when he was thirteen. on the one occasion he felt obliged to return the sentiment, his then girlfriend, amanda[7], stared into his eyes and said she saw nothing but static. that night he drew blood from his wrist and traced the length of her spine with his fingertip as she slept. he never saw her again.

ANNA[8] IS waiting patiently for me upon the cathedral steps, lost in thought and chewing the nail on her little finger. i've noticed the world runs in reverse whenever she is near. objects in my periphery recede and the ground distends with each step. what is dry is eventually wet. soon pools gather, puddles ascend, and the sky struggles to catch the onslaught.

nice day for it.

she tips her nose to the air with a smirk as the rising billows twist and turn around us like swarms of locusts, trawling our serrated contours. when we touch incisions are carved into my skin, pieces of her will migrate into me. those pieces are now many and i'm no longer able to distinguish which is her and which is me. inside, she dances deliriously to the sound of rain, arms aloft, and i feel it reverberate, scaling the walls of my skull,

furiously creating scars.

---

[8] whenever anna is alone a voice echoes somewhere inside of her. it tells her tales of her mother, miriam, who abandoned her when she was five. more often than not these stories have a tragic end, punctuated with a creative variation on the method of death. but sometimes, just sometimes, on a particularly bad day, they conclude with a reunion. today, miriam is driven into the concrete by a plummeting spire seconds before reaching anna's feet.

He was already pulling it from the growing crack in his forearm like a length of vein when she arrived, running her fingers as usual through the wind chimes above the doorframe as she entered.

The touch of cold metal beneath his skin gives him comfort; each morning he'll soak the thin rod in surgical spirit and insert it carefully with a steady, latex gloved hand.

She makes her way over to him now, rolling a spindly index finger over the volume control along the way, and reaches for the already prepared, soaked cotton wool by his side. Droning, aimless bass fills the room as she daubs the exhausted crack and seals in a few uprooted wires tight with a strip of black electrical tape he'd cut earlier, careful not to ash in the opening with her newly sparked cigarette, her first and last of the day.

And then they engage.

RETURN TO SENDER

A last blown kiss hits the still sky like a bullet in a deafening explosion, disfiguring it with a momentary fracture that splinters and gradually disperses, sending a tumbling spent shell back into a weathered, outstretched palm.

HALOS

it fires, propulsive, like semen, into
wet hearts. round after round. and
bodies exhale, feeling the gain.
circular contusions hanging above,
stressed and cracked.

●